CLAIRE *and the* UNICORN
happy ever after

SIMON & SCHUSTER BOOKS FOR YOUNG READERS ✦ An imprint of Simon & Schuster Children's Publishing Division ✦ 1230 Avenue of the Americas, New York, New York 10020 ✦ Text copyright © 2006 by B. G. Hennessy ✦ Illustrations copyright © 2006 by Susan Mitchell ✦ All rights reserved, including the right of reproduction in whole or in part in any form. ✦ SIMON & SCHUSTER BOOKS FOR YOUNG READERS is a trademark of Simon & Schuster, Inc. ✦ Book design by Jessica Sonkin ✦ The text for this book is set in Oneleigh. ✦ The illustrations for this book are rendered in watercolor. ✦ Manufactured in China ✦ 10 9 8 7 6 5 4 3 2 1 ✦ Library of Congress Cataloging-in-Publication Data ✦ Hennessy, B. G. (Barbara G.) ✦ Claire and the unicorn happy ever after / B. G. Hennessy ; illustrated by Susan Mitchell.—1st ed. ✦ p. cm. ✦ Summary: One night, Claire and her toy unicorn, Capricorn, journey to a magical land filled with characters from fairy tales to find out what makes someone live "happy ever after." ✦ ISBN-13: 978-1-4169-0815-9 ✦ ISBN-10: 1-4169-0815-3 ✦ [1. Unicorns—Fiction. 2. Characters in literature—Fiction. 3. Books and reading—Fiction. 4. Toys—Fiction.] I. Mitchell, Susan, 1962– ill. II. Title. ✦ PZ7.H3914Ceh 2006 ✦ [E]—dc22 ✦ 2005002850

For Mackenzie and Simon Cantor—two great kids
—B. G. H.

For Mum, who always believed in dreams
—S. M.

CLAIRE and the UNICORN happy ever after

B. G. Hennessy

ILLUSTRATED BY *Susan Mitchell*

SIMON & SCHUSTER BOOKS FOR YOUNG READERS
New York ◆ London ◆ Toronto ◆ Sydney

"And they lived happily ever after. The end,'" read Claire's dad as he closed the book.

"What made them happy *forever*, Daddy?" Claire asked.

Her dad laughed. "I don't know, Claire; the book doesn't say. Why don't you think about it tonight, and tell me what you come up with in the morning," he said.

Claire plumped up her pillows, pulled up the blanket, and hugged her favorite stuffed animal, Capricorn the unicorn. She closed her eyes, settled back into her pillow, and started thinking about what would make someone happy ever after.

Right in the place about three miles from being awake and two blocks from being asleep, she felt a soft, warm breeze on her face, and the silky feel of Capricorn's back underneath her.

"Hold on tight!" called Capricorn. "Up we go!" And off they went.

Claire felt a little bump as Capricorn's hooves touched the ground. They were in a beautiful forest.

"Let's go ask," said Capricorn.

"Ask who? Ask *what*?" said Claire.

"We will ask whoever we find first what makes them happy," said Capricorn.

"There, ask one of them," said Capricorn.

"Who?" said Claire.

"Why, the fairies of course! There's one, right there above your head. He's the Library Fairy," said Capricorn as he pointed to a tree branch with his horn. Claire's eyes opened wide.

"Good evening, Mr. Fairy," said Claire. "I was wondering, could you tell us what makes someone happy ever after?"

"What kind of someone?" he asked Claire.

"Well, how about you?" asked Claire.

"ME? That's easy," he said. "A good book and some peace and quiet! That's what makes me happy!"

"Well, how about a princess or prince, then?" Claire said. "Hmmmmm. Do I look like a prince or princess?" replied the Library Fairy. "Who is the nearest princess, let me see . . . ," he said, paging through his book. "That would be . . . *p* for 'Princess.' Ah, yes. She would be closest. Try the castle beyond those trees. Tower bedroom, on the left."

"Thank you, Sir Fairy," said Claire.

"Here we go; hold on," warned Capricorn as he leapt up to the tower bedroom balcony.

"Oh, my," said Claire. "I know who *this* princess is."

Capricorn gently tapped on the window with his horn.

"Come in," said the princess.

"Good evening, Miss Princess," Claire said with a curtsy. "Sorry to bother you, but my unicorn and I were wondering if you could tell us what makes a princess happy ever after?"

"I'll tell you what would make *me* happy . . . ," she said.

"A nice, soft, comfortable bed and a good night's sleep! That's what would make me happy! I haven't slept a wink since I got here." And she pulled the covers up right over her head.

"Just a bed?" asked Claire.

"No, not *any* bed. A nice, comfortable, *soft* bed," said the princess. "Not like this pile of rocks that I'm sleeping on!"

"I see," said Claire. "Thank you, Your Highness."

"Maybe we should go ask a prince," Capricorn whispered.

"Pardon me, Miss Princess. Would you happen to know where we might find the nearest prince?" asked Claire.

"Try looking by the pond in the garden," said the princess.

The garden was beautiful, even at night. But they didn't see any prince.

"Maybe he's not here," said Claire.

"He could be at a ball," said Capricorn.

"Who are you looking for?" said a low voice by the pond.

Claire didn't see anybody. "Who said that?" she asked.

"Over here, third lily pad past the bridge," said the voice.

There in the moonlight Claire saw who was speaking. She giggled. "I know who this prince is!" she said, and she pointed to the frog on the lily pad.

"Are you sure he's a *prince*?" asked Capricorn.

"My book said so," said Claire.

"Well, ask him then," said Capricorn.

"Sir Frog, do you know what makes a prince happy ever after?" she asked.

"What makes *me* happiest are nice, big, juicy . . .

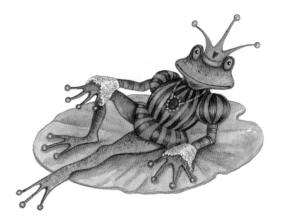

"FLIES!" croaked the Frog Prince. Capricorn and Claire looked at each other.

"Why, yes, I'm sure they do. Thank you, Mr. Prince," said Claire politely.

"Soft beds and juicy flies?" whispered Capricorn. "I'm glad I'm not a prince or a princess!"

"Mr. Prince, could you suggest someone else we might ask?" said Claire.

"Let's see. Who knows about what makes people happy? You could ask Fairy Godmother. She might be able to help you. She should be in the pumpkin patch," croaked the prince as he jumped off his lily pad and back into the pond.

Fairy Godmother was trying out some new spells on the pumpkins.

"Excuse me, ma'am," said Claire. "We were hoping you could help us."

"Why, yes dear, what would you like?" said Fairy Godmother as she pointed her wand at Claire.

"We just have a question," said Claire. "We are wondering if you could tell us what makes someone happy ever after."

Fairy Godmother smiled. "My, my, *that* is an interesting question. I've granted many different wishes in my time—true love, a charming prince, a kind princess, gold, beauty—but come to think of it, I don't believe I've ever heard the same wish twice. But if it is wishes you want to know about, ask the wishing well in the woods."

"I think we will," said Claire. "Thank you very much."

"Hello," Claire called down the wishing well.
"Hello, hello, hello," the wishing well echoed back.
"We have a question, Mr. Well," said Claire.
"Ask away," answered the well. "No charge for questions."
"Can you tell us what makes someone happy ever after?" said Claire.
"My dear, so far I've heard 1,682 wishes and no one has ever asked me that!" gurgled the well. "Do you have an easier question?"
"Not tonight," said Claire, who was getting very sleepy. "Thanks anyway."

"We really didn't get an answer to our question, did we?" said Claire to Capricorn.

"Well, we got *lots* of answers," said Capricorn. "Books, beds, flies, true love, a handsome prince, a kind princess, peace and quiet. Maybe it's one of those questions that doesn't really have just one answer."

The next morning at breakfast Claire's dad asked her if she had figured out what makes someone happy ever after.

"It depends," said Claire.

"On what?" asked her dad.

"On who you are," said Claire. "A very tired princess may just want a comfortable bed. Another princess might be looking for true love. A frog prince would be happy with nice, juicy flies. It all depends," said Claire.

Her dad smiled. "A very wise answer, Claire. Different things do make different people happy, even princes and princesses," he said.

"Now, what would make *my* little princess happy?" he asked.

"Me?" said Claire. "Happy ever after?"

"Well, let's just start with what would make you happy for breakfast," answered her dad.

"How about some pancakes?" said Claire.